SIDNEY
Makes a Wish

First published in 2022 in Great Britain by
Barrington Stoke Ltd
18 Walker Street, Edinburgh, EH3 7LP

www.barringtonstoke.co.uk

A CIP catalogue record for this book is available
from the British Library upon request

ISBN: 978-1-80090-143-8

Printed by Hussar Books, Poland

This book is in a super-readable format for young readers
beginning their independent reading journey.

SIDNEY
Makes a Wish

LISA THOMPSON

Illustrated by
JESS ROSE

Barrington Stoke

For Mum

Contents

Chapter 1

The Wishing Well

One morning when Sidney was on his way to school with his mum, he spotted something hidden in some tall grass.

He went to have a look.

It was a little brick circle with a grey slate roof like a crooked hat.

"What's this, Mum?" he said, patting his hand on the cold bricks.

"That's the old wishing well!" said his mum. "I'd forgotten it was here. When I was little, I threw a penny into the well and made a wish."

Sidney looked down into the dark well and saw the bright blue sky reflected in the rippling water. He sniffed. It smelled of damp things.

"Did your wish come true?" Sidney asked.

His mum smiled at him.

"Of course it did!" she said. "I've got you, haven't I? And you are all of my best wishes come true."

Sidney frowned. *That* wasn't a proper wish!

*

When they got to school, Sidney rushed over to Billy and Austin, who were playing near the PE shed.

Sidney used to be good friends with Billy, but now Billy seemed to want to spend all of his time with Austin.

"Hi, Billy!" said Sidney.

Billy didn't see Sidney standing there.

"Do you want to come over tonight and have a go on my trampoline, Billy?" said Austin.

Billy nodded quickly.

"Yeah!" he said. And he punched the air.

Sidney waited to see if Austin would invite him as well, but just then the bell went for them to line up to go into the classroom.

They all rushed off, and Sidney squeezed in next to Billy. He tapped Billy's back, and Billy turned around.

"You can come to my house one day after school if you want to," said Sidney.

Billy gave a shrug. "Maybe," he said.

Sidney frowned as Billy turned around again. He didn't seem very keen at all.

*

On the way home from school, Sidney and his mum walked past the wishing well hidden behind the tall grass.

"Mum? Do you think the wishing well still works?" said Sidney.

His mum smiled. "I don't see why not," she said.

Sidney was glad about that. He remembered that he had four brown coins sitting on the table by his bed.

He was going to give the wishing well a try.

Chapter 2

The First Wish

The next morning on the walk to school, Sidney ran through the tall grass to the well.

"I'll be just a minute!" he shouted to his mum.

He stood by the wishing well and took a cold brown coin out of his pocket.

He didn't know how you made a wish, but he thought it might be a good idea to close his eyes.

He squeezed his eyes tightly shut but then opened one of them just a little and took a peek.

"I wish," he whispered, just in case his mum could hear, "I wish I had a trampoline as big as three beds!"

He took a deep breath, then let go of the coin.

He waited and waited and waited. At long last, there was a small PLOP.

He felt a little tingle in his toes, and he grinned. The wish must have worked! Sidney had always wanted a trampoline, and now that he was going to get one, he would invite Billy round to play. They would jump and jump for hours and hours, and then Billy would think that Sidney was the BEST friend in the world.

When he got to school, he planned to tell Billy all about the trampoline, but Billy was running races with Austin, and Sidney couldn't catch them.

He gave up and stood by his mum as she chatted with Carrie's dad. Carrie hadn't been at Sidney's school for very long.

"Hi, Sidney!" said Carrie, peeping out at him from behind her dad.

"Hmmm," said Sidney.

He didn't really want to talk to Carrie. He was too busy watching Billy and Austin and wishing that he could join in.

*

After school, Sidney couldn't wait to get home to jump on his brand-new trampoline.

His mum unlocked the front door, and he ran through the house to the garden.

But when he got there, everything was just as before.

The lawn still had brown patches, the fence was still wonky, and there was definitely no trampoline.

The wish hadn't worked.

Chapter 3

An Ice-Cream Machine

In school the next day, Sidney thought about his wish. Maybe the trampoline was just TOO BIG and that was why it hadn't worked? Maybe he should make a smaller wish. The wishing well was only little, after all.

At playtime, he skipped over to Billy.

"Hi, Billy," he said. "Do you want to play pirates?"

Pirates was always their favourite game of all.

"I guess we could," said Billy. But then Austin ran up and threw his arm around Billy.

"Hey, Billy," Austin said. "My mum's going to take us to get ice creams after school!"

"Oh wow!" said Billy. He and Austin both "whooped", then sped off around the playground.

Sidney wanted to get an ice cream too. He felt very sad and left out. He had seen the big metal ice-cream machine with a pink handle in the ice-cream shop. He sighed to himself. Billy and Austin were going to have such a good time.

*

On the way home from school, Sidney's mum stopped to talk to Carrie's dad.

Carrie was holding on to her dad's hand. They were standing right by the wishing well.

"Hi, Sidney," said Carrie. "School was good, wasn't it?"

"Um. Yes. It was OK," said Sidney. He didn't want to talk to Carrie right now. He had something he needed to do.

Sidney's fingers found another brown coin in his pocket, and he skipped over to the wishing well.

"I wish," he whispered. "I wish I had my very own ice-cream machine! A shiny metal one with a little pink handle like the one in the ice-cream shop!"

He took a deep breath, then let go of the coin. Down and down into the well it dropped.

Sidney waited and waited and waited.

At last, there was a small PLOP.

He felt a little tingle in his fingers, and he wiggled them. This wish had worked for sure!

If he had an ice-cream machine, he could invite Billy over and they would eat loads and loads of ice cream. They would be best friends for ever!

He ran back to his mum, and Carrie grinned at him.

"What did you wish for, Sidney?" Carrie said.

She must have been watching him!

Sidney couldn't tell her what he had wished for. Everyone knew that if you told someone your wish, it didn't come true. That was the basic rule of wishing.

"Nothing," he said.

Carrie gave a shrug and started talking about her rabbits, but Sidney

wasn't really listening. He was too
busy thinking about his new ice-cream
machine.

*

As soon as his mum unlocked the front
door, Sidney rushed to the kitchen. But
when he got there, the kitchen looked
exactly the same as it had done that
morning.

On the counter was their old kettle.
Next to the kettle were two mugs that
had MUM and SIDNEY written on them.

And there was definitely no
ice-cream machine.

Why hadn't the wish worked?

Sidney thought about his wish. He'd already worked out that the trampoline was too big for a wish, so maybe an ice-cream maker was too messy? Yes, that was why it hadn't worked. The wish was too messy!

Chapter 4

The Robot Dog

The next day, Carrie and her dad were waiting at the end of Sidney's garden so they could all walk to school together.

"Did your wish come true, Sidney?" said Carrie.

Sidney shook his head. "No, it didn't," he said. "I don't know what I'm doing wrong. I've closed my eyes without peeking, I've not told anyone what I've wished for, AND I've wished really hard. And now I've only got two coins left!"

He let out a deep breath. It felt good to tell Carrie. Maybe she'd know how to get the wishing well to work.

"Hmmm," said Carrie, brushing her hand along a hedge as she walked. "Maybe you're not wishing for the right thing?"

Not wishing for the right thing? thought Sidney. What did that mean?

He really wanted the trampoline, and he really wanted the metal ice-cream machine.

Billy would have loved them both, and then they'd be best friends again!

Then another idea popped into his head. Last year, Billy had told him about a robot dog that he'd seen on TV. He had talked about it all the time, and he had said that he was going to save his pocket money and buy one. But he never did.

And now Sidney could wish for one!

"You're right, Carrie!" said Sidney with a big smile. "I know exactly what to wish for now!"

Carrie smiled back at him.

Sidney skipped over to the wishing well and took a coin from his pocket. He closed his eyes tightly shut.

"I wish ..." he whispered, "I wish I had a robot dog."

In his head he could see a picture
of a little blue dog with a remote control
that you used to make it walk, yap, sit
and beg.

The robot dog wasn't too big, and it wasn't messy. And the most important thing was that Billy would *definitely* love it! It was the perfect wish.

Sidney took a deep breath, then let go of the coin and waited and waited and waited. At last, there was a small PLOP.

He felt a tingle on the very tip of his nose, and he rubbed it. This time the wish had worked! He was sure of it.

He would invite Billy over, and they would play together with the dog and be best friends.

He ran back to where Carrie stood.
Was she going to ask him what he wished
for again? No, she didn't – she just
swung her arms and hopped in zigzags
now and then as they walked along.

Chapter 5

Is the Wishing Well Broken?

School went on and on and on. It always did that when Sidney really wanted it to end.

At playtime, he spotted Billy with a group of boys in the corner of the playground.

Sidney went over and stood beside them. They were talking about a film they had all seen at the cinema, but Sidney hadn't seen it, so he found it hard to join in.

When the bell went to say it was the end of playtime, Sidney caught up with Billy.

"Do you still like dogs, Billy?" said Sidney. "I don't mean real ones. I mean robot ones. Where you can control them yourself with a remote."

Billy looked at him and frowned.

"What *are* you talking about?" he said. He didn't sound friendly at all.

"I'm getting a robot dog," Sidney went on, as if Billy was still his friend. "You can come round and see it if you like?"

Billy frowned at him again.

"Remember you saw one on TV once and you wanted to buy it?" said Sidney.

Billy grinned. "Oh yeah," he said. "I liked those when I was little." He then walked off and said something to one of the other boys. They all started laughing.

Sidney didn't say anything. He lined up with everyone else and went inside.

Suddenly, he felt a tap on his arm. It was Carrie.

"I like robot dogs," said Carrie.

She must have been listening.

"I've got a wind-up chicken," Carrie said. "You turn a little key, and it walks around and pecks at the ground. It's really funny."

Sidney thought about the wind-up chicken. It sounded interesting but not as exciting as his robot dog.

"Oh," said Sidney. "That's nice."

Carrie smiled.

*

On the way home from school, Sidney walked as quickly as he could.

"What's the hurry, Sidney?" said his mum.

"Nothing, Mum," said Sidney.

He did think about telling her about the brand-new robot dog waiting for him at home, but he didn't. Just in case it stopped the wish from coming true.

As soon as his mum unlocked the door, Sidney rushed inside.

He held out his arms, ready to pick up the dog, but there was nothing there. Not even a cardboard box with a robot dog inside.

He sat on the floor feeling very sad.

Why wasn't the wishing well working? Was it broken? It just didn't make any sense! And now he only had one coin left. The next wish had to be the best one yet.

Chapter 6

The Last Wish

The next morning, Carrie and her dad weren't waiting for them at the end of their garden, so Sidney and his mum walked to school on their own.

"Are you OK, Sidney?" said his mum. "You're very quiet today."

Sidney held the coin tightly in his fist.

"I'm just thinking about the wishing well," said Sidney. "I don't think it's working like it did when you were little."

His mum stopped to look down at Sidney, and she gave his hand a squeeze.

"Sometimes we wish for things and we don't see that we already have exactly what we want, right there in front of us," she said.

That didn't make any sense.

The trampoline, the ice-cream maker and the robot dog – he didn't have any of those things! And he really wanted them!

But when he thought about it a bit more, he realised that he hadn't really ever wanted those things for himself. He had just wished for them to make Billy his friend again.

So what was the thing that *Sidney* really wanted?

They got to the wishing well, and Sidney gripped on to the last coin in his pocket.

"I'll just be a minute, Mum," he said.

He ran through the long grass, then closed his eyes and held the brown coin between his finger and thumb.

This was it. This was his last chance of a wish from the wishing well.

He now knew exactly what he wanted. In fact, it had been his wish all along. It had just been hidden by the other wishes.

"I wish," he whispered, "I wish I had my very own friend."

He opened his eyes, looked down into the deep well and got ready to let go of the very last coin.

But just then another face popped up opposite his reflection in the dark rippling water. Sidney blinked.

"Hi, Sidney," the face said.

Sidney looked up. Standing across from him was Carrie.

"Hi, Carrie," said Sidney. He kept hold of his coin.

She scuffed her foot along the ground and didn't look at him.

"My dad is asking your mum if you can come over to play tonight," said Carrie. "Would you like to?"

Sidney looked at Carrie. Was she really inviting him round to play? *That would be cool*, he thought.

"Um. OK," he said. "Sure! I'd like that."

Carrie looked up and smiled.

"Good! You can meet my rabbits! Do you like rabbits?" she asked.

Sidney gave a shrug. "I don't know," he said. "I've never met one."

Carrie thought that was really funny, and she laughed and Sidney laughed too.

"Come on, you two," called Sidney's mum. "Let's get to school."

Sidney and Carrie skipped over to their parents, and Sidney slipped the dark brown coin back into his pocket.

He didn't need the last wish after all.